J.J. and WASHI MACHINE

Firefly

First published in 1990 by
Firefly Books Limited
61 Western Road, Hove,
East Sussex BN3 1JD

© Copyright 1990 Firefly Books Limited

© Copyright Susan Field (text and illustrations)

This edition published in 1991 by
Firefly Books Limited

Editor: Francesca Motisi

British Library Cataloguing in Publication Data
Field, Susan
    JJ and the washing machine.
    I. Title   II. Series
    823.914 [J]

    ISBN 1-85485-166-7

Typeset by
DP Press Limited, Sevenoaks, Kent
Manufactured in Italy by G. Canale & C. S.p.A., Borgaro T.se - Turin

J.J. and the WASHING MACHINE

Written and Illustrated
by Susan Anna Field

For JJ and Jem

In the whole of the kitchen, the washing machine was JJ's favourite thing. He had great fun helping to load it . . .

And helping to empty it . . . In between loading
and emptying, he would just sit and watch the
clothes go round and round inside. He could
watch it for ages – sometimes for a whole five
minutes, and it made some wonderful noises like:
    SLOSHETY-SLOSHETY-SLOSH and
    GURGLE-McWHURGLE-McGLUB-GLUB
and
    CHUGGA-CHUGGA-CHUGGA and
    CLICKETY-CLICKETY-VROOOM
Last of all it would go round very, very fast with
a noise like WHEEEEEEEEE! Only much
louder than I could ever say it.

One day, JJ was in the kitchen when he heard someone say, 'Ahem.'

He knew that mummy was upstairs talking on the 'phone, so he wondered where the 'Ahem' could have come from. He looked around but no one was there. Very strange.

　　'Ahem,' said someone again.

　　'Who's that?' said JJ.

　　'Me,' came the reply.

　　'Who's me?' asked JJ.

　　'The washing machine,' said the washing machine.

JJ's eyes grew very wide indeed. He wasn't sure whether this was a normal thing to happen and approached the washing machine, very carefully. 'Hello washing machine!' he said.

'Actually the name's Kenneth,' said the
washing machine, 'but you can call me Ken.'
'Hello Ken' said JJ.
'Hello JJ' said Ken.

'I've been wanting to ask you for some time now,' said Ken, 'whether you would mind me having a look around your garden. You see, I haven't been out of the kitchen for such a long time and I'd love to get some fresh air.'

'Why of course you can Ken,' said JJ. And together they went out into the garden.

In the garden they looked at the big,
shiny red poppies and little white flowers;
at bees going BUZZZZ and at the
insects creepy-crawlying around.

They saw birds hopping in the
branches of the trees and they also saw
the neighbour's cat which was digging
holes in the flower-bed, as usual! Ken
was very excited and kept blowing clouds
of bubbles into the air.

JJ was getting very involved with the creepy-crawly things, when he noticed that the cat had stopped in the middle of digging a hole and was looking at something with a very worried expression on its face.

JJ looked up just in time to see Ken wandering out through the gate, trailing his lead behind him. JJ knew that he was not really allowed to go out through the gate without an adult, but he thought that his mum would probably be quite cross if he told her that the washing machine had just walked out.

In fact he suspected that she might not believe him. There was nothing for it but to try and get Ken back again.

Quick as a flash, JJ grabbed hold of the
lead and tried to pull Ken back. Ken,
however, seemed to be in a daydream.
He was wandering along, whistling a
tune to himself and puffing out more
clouds of bubbles.

Ken was far too strong for JJ, whose
feet kept losing their grip so that he was
dragged along the pavement. His
friends, Jessica and Lucille, attracted by
the clouds of bubbles, were looking over
their garden wall.

'What's happening JJ? What are you doing with that washing machine?' called Jessica.

'Come and help!' shouted JJ, 'I think Ken's trying to run away and mum will be really cross if I don't get him back home soon!' In an instant, Jessica and Lucille were hanging on to the lead with JJ. But even with three of them (or two-and-a-half as Lucille was still rather small to be much help), they couldn't hold Ken back.

As they went up the road, more and more
children ran to help. By the time they reached the
top of the road where the shops were, JJ, Jessica
and Lucille had been joined by Ben, Holly, Jake,
Jasmin, Rose, Thomas, Sharon and Harry, but
they still couldn't make the washing machine stop.
It seemed that Ken didn't even notice the children
hanging on grimly behind him.

'I wonder where he's going?' said Jessica.

Her question was soon answered as Ken
suddenly turned in through an open doorway.

They were in . . . the launderette!
  'Hello everyone!' said Ken.
  'Hello Ken,' said all the washing machines.
They were obviously very happy to see him and
a great cloud of bubbles soon filled the shop.

Mrs Dryer who looked after the launderette didn't seem at all pleased. In fact, she seemed to be rather frightened by the celebrations which were going on and ran out of the shop shouting, 'Help! Help! My washing machines are having a party!'

Meanwhile, the children's parents had gathered, having noticed that their children had disappeared. They were just about to call the police when they saw Mrs Dryer running towards them.

In no time they were all inside the launderette.
At first none of the mums or dads looked at all
happy. But when Ken said how sorry he was for
causing so much trouble, and promised not to go

wandering off again, they all forgave him and
cheered up.

'I think we'd better go home now,' said JJ's mum,
'and you are all invited to our house for tea.'

So, Jessica, Lucille, Ben, Holly, Jake, Jasmin, Rose, Thomas, Sharon, Harry and all their mums and dads squeezed into JJ's house for tea, and because there weren't enough seats for everyone, JJ sat very comfortably on top of his new friend – the washing machine.

THE END